Disney's

THE
LION KING

Ladybird

Under a cold starlit sky, the African plain lay quiet, waiting for the sun to rise.

As the first bright rays appeared, animals popped up here and there, birds took to the air, and insects came out of hiding. Soon a whole parade of animals marched across the vast Pride Lands. There were elephants, rhinos, giraffes and ostriches, cheetahs, ants and chattering baboons. Their journey was long, and the sun grew hotter, shining down from a cloudless sky.

Today was a very important day, and everyone was excited. They were going to see their new prince for the first time. He was Simba, son of Queen Sarabi and King Mufasa, the Lion King who ruled the Pride Lands.

At last the animals reached Pride Rock and waited patiently.

Rafiki, an ancient, mystic baboon, gave the new cub his blessing. Then, holding him high, he cried out, "We welcome Simba, our future king, to the Circle of Life."

The animals cheered and shouted in reply, "Welcome, Prince Simba, welcome!"

Once the ceremony was over, King Mufasa went to see his younger brother, Scar. His adviser, Zazu, went with him.

"Is anything wrong, Scar?" asked the king. "Queen Sarabi and I were disappointed not to see you at Simba's presentation this morning." Scar looked away and said nothing. There *was* something wrong. The only thing he had ever really wanted was to be king himself, and now the new cub's arrival had spoiled his chances. "Oh, sorry," he mused. "It must have slipped my mind."

"As the king's brother, you should have been first in line," said Zazu.

"I was first in line," snarled Scar, "until that little hairball was born." And he began to walk away in disgust.

Now King Mufasa grew angry. "Don't turn your back on me, Scar," he ordered.

Scar faced his brother. "Oh, no! Perhaps you shouldn't turn your back on me, Mufasa!"

The king bristled and seemed to grow larger.

"Are you threatening me, Scar?" he demanded, taking a step forward.

But Scar paid no attention. He stalked away without replying.

Soon Prince Simba was exploring the Pride Lands. Sometimes he went with his father and sometimes with his best friend, Nala, a lioness cub. But there was one place the cubs were not allowed to go – the shadowy land beyond the northern border. Mufasa would only say that it was too dangerous.

But Simba's scheming Uncle Scar was keen to tell him. "It's an elephant graveyard," he explained. "And only the bravest lions can go there."

"I'm brave," thought Simba. "And I'm going to prove it to Father."

Today Zazu was keeping an eye on the two cubs. "Come on, Nala," said Simba. "We're going to the elephant graveyard." And they scampered off.

Zazu started after them, but they were soon out of sight. He caught up at the edge of the border and squawked, "We're in great danger. We must leave here right now."

Just then, three giggling hyenas poked their heads out of an elephant skull. Simba tried to roar, but it sounded more like a squeak. But a huge ROARRR! split the air. The hyenas looked round – straight into the eyes of Mufasa. "It's the king!" they yelled. "Let's get out of here."

Later, when they were alone, the king said, "I'm disappointed in you, Simba. You could have been killed. So could Nala and Zazu."

Simba hung his head in shame. "I'm sorry, Father," he said. Then he struggled to explain. "I was just trying to be brave like you."

"Being brave doesn't mean you go looking for trouble," said Mufasa. "Today I was scared, because I thought I might lose you. Now, let's go home. Your mother will be worried."

As they made their way back, they watched the sky fill with stars. Simba asked, "Father, we'll always be together, won't we?"

His father stopped and spoke gently. "Simba, let me tell you something my father told me long ago. Look up at the stars." Simba gazed upwards obediently.

"The great kings of the past look down on us from those stars," said Mufasa. "They are part of the great Circle of Life. They will always be there to guide you – and so will I. Remember that."

"I will," promised Simba.

Scar wasted no time in setting up a new plan with the hyenas.
"You lost a great opportunity yesterday," he told them. "You could
have got rid of Simba and Mufasa! Now, listen very carefully.
I have another plan…"

*   *   *

The next morning, Scar led Simba down into a deep
gorge. Simba was puzzled, but his uncle explained,
"Your father has a wonderful surprise for you.
Just stay here for a moment." Then he hurried away.

At Scar's signal, the hyenas charged into the
middle of a herd of wildebeest. The huge
animals began to stampede – and Simba
was right in their path! He clawed his
way onto a branch above them –
but the branch cracked.

Devious Scar knew Mufasa and Zazu
were walking nearby. He dashed
up to them, yelling,
"There's a stampede
in the gorge and
Simba's trapped!"

"I'm coming, son,"
shouted Mufasa and he
raced to Simba's rescue.

The king battled through the galloping beasts and grabbed Simba in his mouth. He carried him to the safety of a rocky ledge. But as Mufasa tried to pull himself to the top of the gorge, he saw his brother looking down at him. "Scar, help me!" he cried.

Scar leaned over and snarled, "Long live the king!" Then he gave Mufasa a deadly push. His brother fell down to the bottom of the gorge and lay still.

As soon as the wildebeest had gone, Simba ran to Mufasa. "Father! Father!" he cried. But there was no reply. Simba nuzzled the lifeless body.

Just then Scar appeared. "This is *your* fault," he said grimly. "If the king hadn't tried to save you, he'd still be alive. You must leave the Pride Lands and never return."

Sobbing, Simba fled.

Scar told the hyenas to follow and kill the cub. He himself went back to Pride Rock triumphant – the king and his son were dead.

But the rest of the pride were devastated.

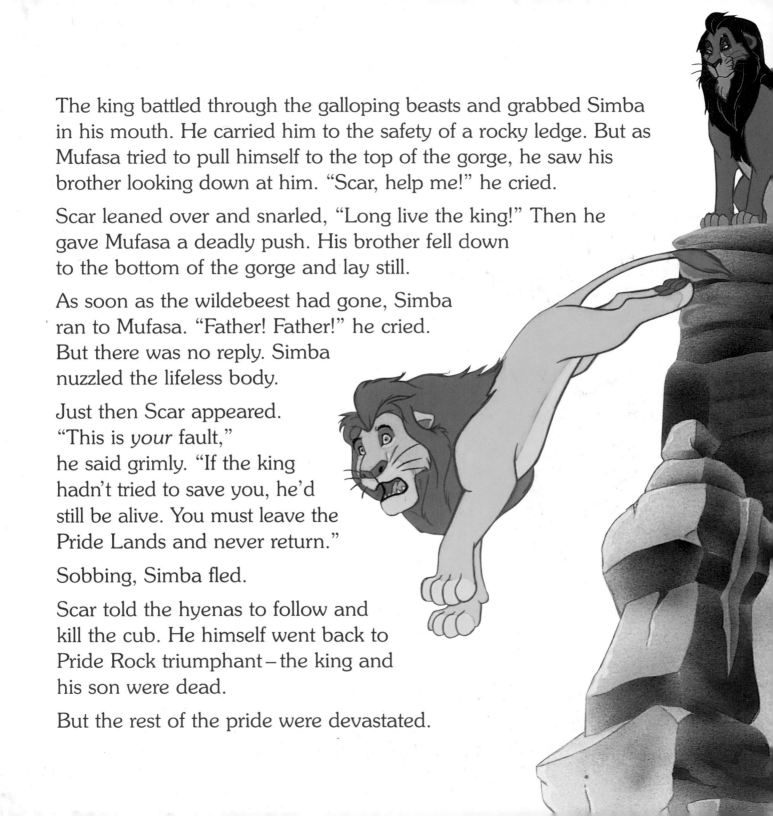

Scar didn't know it, but his nephew wasn't dead. The hyenas had given up the chase. And as Scar proclaimed himself king, Simba lay on the ground exhausted. The hot sun beat down, and vultures circled hopefully above him.

When Simba eventually opened his eyes, he saw a meerkat and a warthog watching him. "You nearly died!" said the warthog. "We saved you."

"Thanks for your help," said Simba, standing up shakily. "I have to go now." And he turned to walk away.

"Where are you going?" asked the meerkat.

"I don't know," said Simba. "I can't go back home."

"Don't worry," said the meerkat. "Put your past behind you. Hakuna Matata! No worries, no responsibilities. That's how we like to live! Why don't you stay with us?"

"My name's Pumbaa," said the warthog, "and this is Timon."

Simba thought about it. Why not? He had nowhere else to go. "I will. Thanks!" he said.

When Simba looked at the jungle round him, he was surprised. It was nothing like living on the open plain. There were leaves everywhere, and it was cool beneath the trees. High above them noisy parrots and chattering monkeys searched for fruit and nuts.

Timon showed him their home behind a huge fern. Simba peeped in. "It's beautiful," he said. "Do you live here all the time?"

"We live wherever we want to, and do whatever we want to," said Timon. "Hakuna Matata – no worries at all. You'll love it here. Come on, we'll find you some food."

Timon and Pumbaa hunted around on the jungle floor until they found a fallen log. Pumbaa pushed it with his snout, and Timon felt beneath it. "Enough for us all!" he grinned.

Simba wasn't at all keen to try the juicy bugs he was offered. But when he tasted them, he found they were certainly filling and not nearly as bad as he had expected.

It wasn't long before Simba felt at home in the jungle with his new friends. Hakuna Matata – no worries – was a good way to live.

Days became weeks, weeks became months, and months became years. Simba grew into a strong young lion with a handsome mane. The jungle life suited him, and he was happy. He hardly ever thought about the lion pride on the plain. But then a morning came that was to change his life again.

Timon and Pumbaa were searching for bugs and Pumbaa soon found some ants under a thornbush. "Over here, Timon," he cried.

A twig broke behind him, and Pumbaa looked round. But it wasn't Timon. It was a lioness, and she looked hungry. "Help!" yelled Pumbaa. Timon came running, and luckily Simba had heard him too. He shot from the bushes and struggled with the lioness. They wrestled to and fro, then the lioness stopped. "Simba?" she asked. "Nala!" he answered happily.

Timon and Pumbaa watched in surprise as the lions hugged each other, overjoyed. "Hey, what's going on?" they asked.

Nala looked at Simba. "You're alive! And that means you're king! Scar let the hyenas take over. There's no food, no water. You *must* come back and take your rightful place."

"I can never go back," said Simba sadly, and he walked away.

That night, Simba gazed up at the starlit sky. "Even if they are in trouble, I can never go back. I am not you, Father. I never will be."

He turned to see an old, old baboon at his side. "I am Rafiki," said the baboon. "I know your father. I will take you to him."

"But my father is dead!" said Simba in disbelief.

"Just come with me," answered Rafiki.

He followed the baboon to a clear, still pool, and Rafiki told him to look down into the water. At first Simba saw his own reflection. But then the water rippled in the breeze, and when the pool stilled again, Simba saw his father's face.

"You see? Your father lives in you," said Rafiki. "Now, look up!"

A deep voice echoed in the sky, "Simba! Look inside yourself. You must take your place in the great Circle of Life. You are my son, and the one true king. Remember…"

The image faded, Rafiki disappeared and Simba was alone once more.

Next morning Nala, Timon and Pumbaa learnt that Simba had returned to Pride Rock. They decided to follow him.

Meanwhile, back at Pride Rock, Scar was giving orders to Sarabi. All at once, a mighty roar interrupted him. He swung round to see a great lion standing on the cliff. "Mufasa?" he gasped.

But Sarabi recognised Simba straightaway. "My son!" she cried. "You're alive!"

"Yes, and I'm here to take my place as king," said Simba. Scar just jeered and set the hyenas on him.

Simba was forced back over the edge and he clung to the cliff with his claws. "Now," sneered Scar, "where have I seen this before? Oh, I remember – your father looked like this just before I killed him."

Knowing the truth at last gave Simba new strength. He heaved himself up and leapt at his uncle.

As Simba challenged Scar, lightning set the dry grass of the plain on fire, and flames swept towards Pride Rock. Scar lunged round to strike Simba's back. But he missed. Scar fell right over the cliff, to the hyenas below.

Simba roared in triumph from the top of Pride Rock, and it started to rain. Soon the plain began to flourish and there was food for everyone once more.

Simba made Nala his Queen, and before long they had a cub. Early one morning, all the animals gathered again at the foot of Pride Rock. Simba, Nala and their friends watched Rafiki. He lifted the new royal cub towards the sky. All the animals fell silent as they bowed to their future ruler.

Simba remembered his father's wisdom. And with happiness in his heart, he welcomed his own cub into the Circle of Life.